CHANGING

To Ushi (MK)
To Ruby, with love (NM)

GIANTS
Mij Kelly and Nick Maland

First published in 2007 by Hodder Children's Books
First published in paperback in 2008

Text copyright © Mij Kelly 2007
Illustration copyright © Nick Maland 2007

Hodder Children's Books
338 Euston Road, London, NW1 3BH

Hodder Children's Books Australia
Level 17/207 Kent Street, Sydney, NSW 2000

A catalogue record of this book is available
from the British Library.

ISBN: 978 0340 89331 9

10 9 8 7 6 5 4 3 2 1

Colour Reproduction by Dot Gradations Ltd, UK
Printed in China

Hodder Children's Books is a division
of Hachette Children's Books
An Hachette Livre UK Company

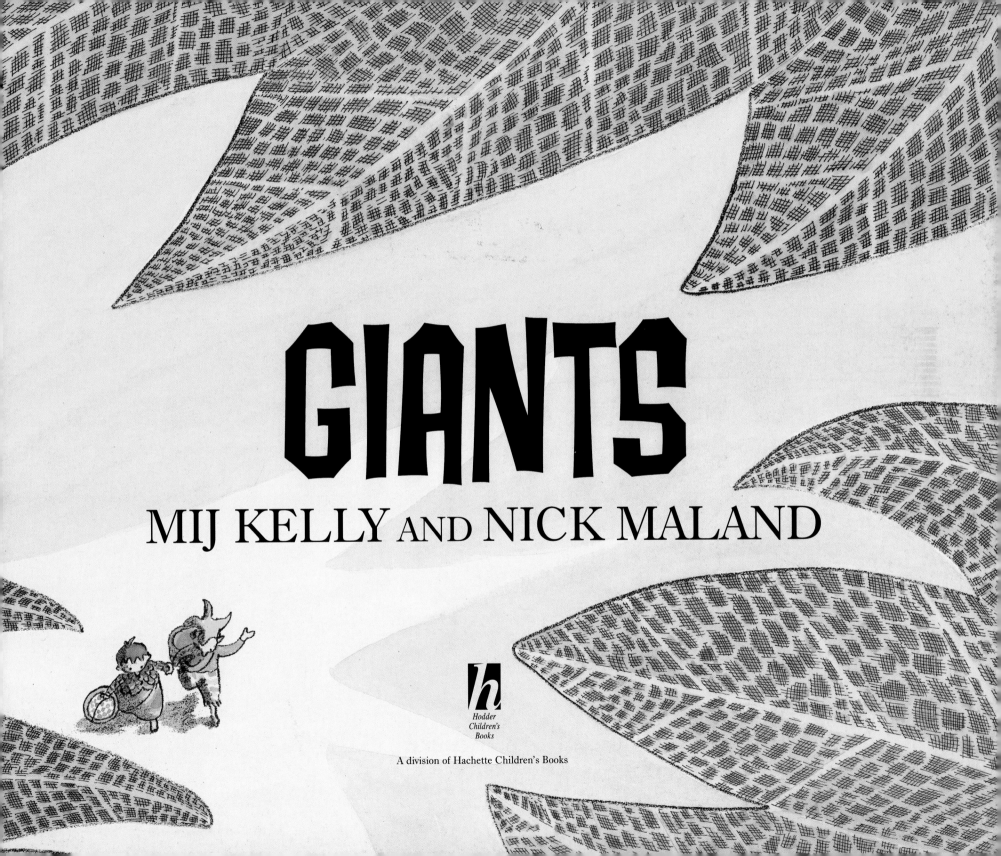

GIANTS

MIJ KELLY AND NICK MALAND

Hodder
Children's
Books

A division of Hachette Children's Books

Sweet Pea and Boogaloo walked under the trees,
under the sun and the green leaves.
They walked and they talked, just like me and you,
and suddenly – quite out of the blue – Sweet Pea said:

'Giants!'

'Giants,' said Sweet Pea.
'Do they look like you and me?
Except bigger?'

'Oh no,' said Boogaloo.
'Giants are nothing like me and you!

They're revolting creatures.
They have hideous features.
They have far too many teeth
sticking out of their jaws and their
hands are like claws.'

'Oh,' said Sweet Pea. 'I see.'

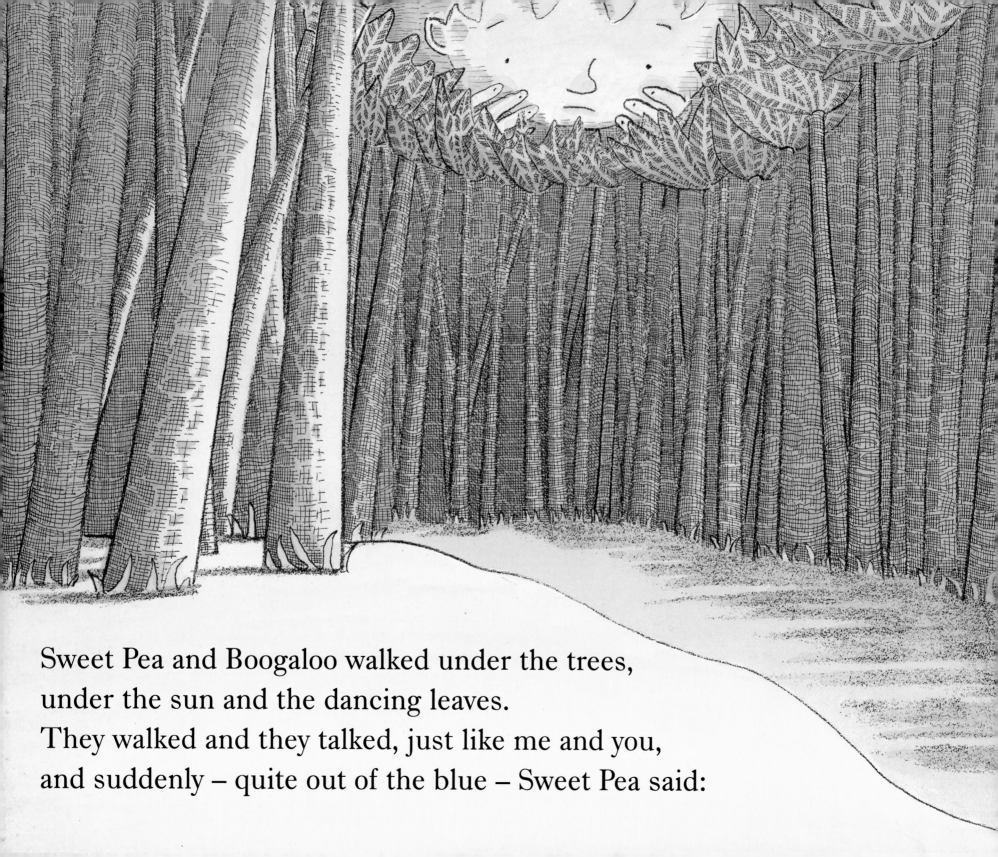

Sweet Pea and Boogaloo walked under the trees,
under the sun and the dancing leaves.
They walked and they talked, just like me and you,
and suddenly – quite out of the blue – Sweet Pea said:

'Are giants kind?'

'Are you out of your mind?'
said Boogaloo.

'Giants are **horrible** through
and through. They don't lift a finger to
help me and you.'

'Oh,' said Sweet Pea.
'I see.'

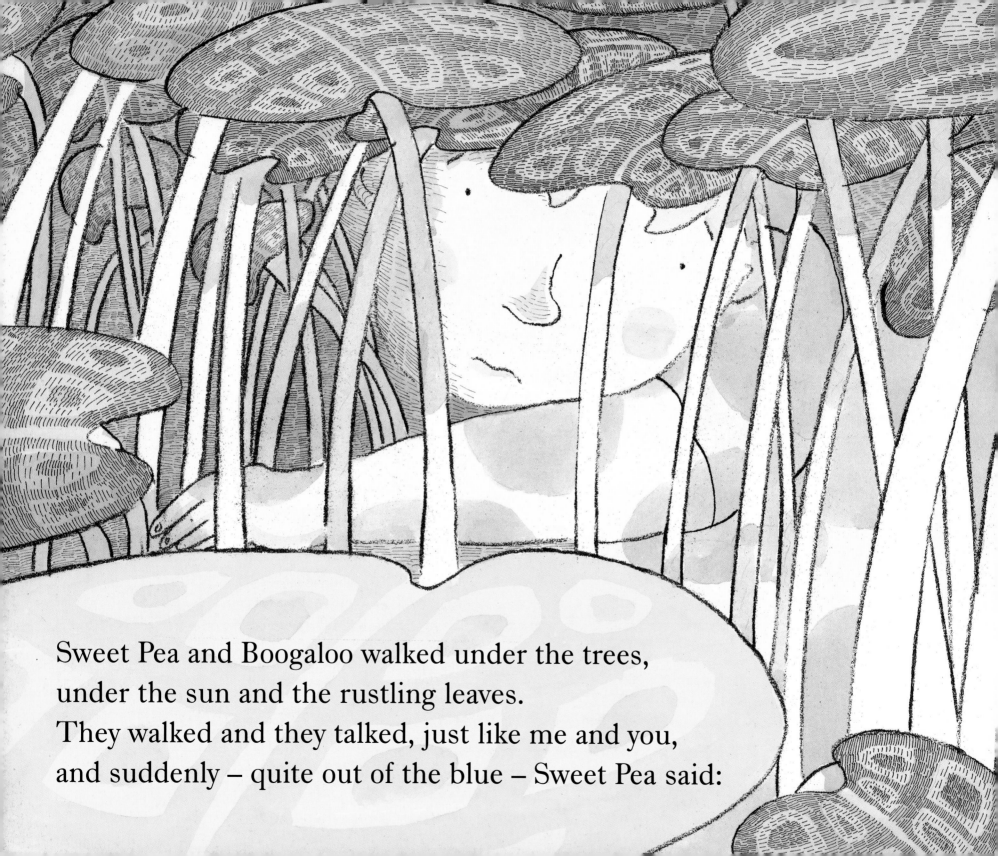

Sweet Pea and Boogaloo walked under the trees,
under the sun and the rustling leaves.
They walked and they talked, just like me and you,
and suddenly – quite out of the blue – Sweet Pea said:

'What do giants eat, Boogaloo?
Do they eat the same things we do?'

'Well I don't like to say,' said Boogaloo.
'But what giants like to eat is…

…me and **you**.'

And Sweet Pea said:
'Are you sure, Boogaloo?'

Under the trees, where the sunlight dapples the forest floor,
Sweet Pea and Boogaloo walked some more.

They talked some more.

Then suddenly – quite out of the blue – Sweet Pea said:

'Do giants have feelings like you and me?'

'About as much feeling as this here tree,' said Boogaloo.

And the giant fell down with a great boo-hoo!

'Now you listen to me!' yelled Sweet Pea.
'It's all lies about giants. It's all untrue.
This giant has feelings just like you.
And you've hurt his feelings, Boogaloo!

Now what are you going to do?'

Poor Boogaloo.
It was all such a shock,
he didn't know what to do.
But he held out his hand
and said: 'How d'you do?

We're going for a picnic.
Do you want to come too?'

Under the trees, under the sun-dappled leaves,
they gave the giant cake and strawberry tea.
They sat on his knee and told him
stories – just like we do.

'I'm sorry,' said Boogaloo, 'but I never met a giant until I met you.'

Just then another giant loomed into view.

She was in such a rush, she had so many things to do – that she almost trod on Boogaloo.

Sweet Pea and Boogaloo hid
under the trees, in the dark
shadow of the rustling leaves.
They hid and they whispered
like we sometimes do.

The giant pulled on his socks
and buckled his shoes...

And stepped out into his world...

just like me and you.